FIGHTING BACK

Amita heard voices outside in the street. Loud, drunk voices, laughing and singing. For a moment, she felt a rising terror. She started to shake with fear. Plucking up courage, she slipped out of bed and peered out of the window. Two young men were winding their way down the street. She could see their football scarves quite clearly as they passed under the lights.

She forced herself to calm down. They were harmless. She was being silly. It couldn't happen here…

Look out for other exciting stories
in the *Shades* series:

FIGHTING BACK

Helen Bird

Evans

Published by Evans Brothers Limited
2A Portman Mansions
Chiltern St
London W1U 6NR

First published in 2005

British Library Cataloguing in Publication Data
Bird, Helen
Fighting Back. - (Shades)
1. Young adult fiction
I. Title
823. 9'2 [J]

ISBN 0 237 52845 2

Series Editor: David Orme
Editor: Julia Moffatt
Designer: Rob Walster
Thanks to Shazia Hadi

Contents

Chapter One
A New Start

Amita followed the Deputy Head along the corridor. It didn't seem too bad. It was neat and clean, brighter than her old school, even in the gloom of late January. Her father hadn't looked pleased, but nothing pleased him these days.

A classroom door opened and a boy came out. He had a self-satisfied smirk on his face. She could hear a raised voice from inside the room.

The boy looked Amita up and down.

'Nice,' he said loudly. 'Very tasty!'

Amita was glad her father had already left. She blushed and turned her face away. The teacher glared at the boy.

'I'll talk to you later,' she said as she went through the door. The boy pretended to shake as if he was afraid.

Amita followed her into the room.

'This is Mrs Soames, your form tutor.' She looked at the teacher. 'You've had all the information, haven't you? Amita will be in top sets for English, Maths and Science.'

Amita looked round the class. A blur of faces. Some looked friendly, others just stared at her. There were several Asians, including a couple of girls wearing veils.

The Deputy Head went out, closing the

door firmly behind her. She stopped to speak to the boy who had been sent out.

'Go and sit with Catherine,' said Mrs Soames. She pointed to a very blonde girl sitting in the middle of the room. 'You're in the same sets as her. She'll give you a copy of your timetable and show you where to go.'

There was a snort of laughter from the back of the room.

'I'll show her where to go if you like miss!'

'Be quiet Tony, I'm not talking to you.' A girl leant over to Tony and whispered something. He gave another snort.

The teacher ignored them and looked down at the register.

'Right. Settle down Year 10. Now, there are a couple of notices. Pay attention. Tony! Sit down and face the front. Maddy, turn round please.'

'Just like my old school,' thought Amita,

as she tried to follow what Catherine was telling her.

A bell rang and Catherine led her off to the first lesson.

'Everybody calls me Cath, not Catherine,' she said. 'Except my mum, of course. She's fussy, but aren't they all?'

Amita liked Cath. The teachers seemed nice too, and the work was interesting. She decided that school was going to be OK.

The morning went very quickly and soon it was lunchtime.

'We've got half an hour tutor time next,' said Cath. 'It's the worst part of the day.'

'Why?'

'Because of Brian and the others. They're just so stupid.'

'Who's Brian?'

'He got sent out just as you came in,' said Cath. 'He's always getting sent out but it doesn't make any difference. There's him, Tony, Maddy, and Luke. They mess around all the time.'

Back in their tutor room Amita soon understood what Cath meant.

'Settle down. *Now!*' Mrs Soames raised her voice above the hubbub.

'This week we're going to be working on the citizenship module.'

'What's that then?' called Tony Banks.

'I know; it's about immigrants,' said Brian, nodding towards a thin boy sitting by himself in one corner.

Amita looked at Brian in surprise. He noticed her glance.

'What about you then? Where're you from?'

'Lancashire.'

'Where's that then? India?'

'No! It's in England. Up North.'

'That's why you talk funny then.'

'He should talk,' whispered Cath. But Brian was off again.

'Why don't you dress like them then?' He pointed to the two Muslim girls.

'Because I'm a Hindu, not a Muslim.'

'So? It's all foreign innit? My dad says you should all go home.'

'That's enough!' Mrs Soames moved to the middle of the room. 'For your information Brian, citizenship is about responsibility as much as anything. If you listen and try and take a proper part in the lesson you might even learn something.'

She started giving out worksheets, then went back to the front and began to lecture the class. They settled down, more or less, and Amita turned round to Cath.

'Why's he going on about immigrants? He's black.'

'Be quiet please, get on with your work.' said Mrs Soames to the class in general. For a while there was relative peace and quiet.

Maddy Smith decided that it had been quiet long enough.

' 'Ere,' she said to Amita, 'Luke fancies you – d'you wanna go out with 'im?'

'Just ignore them all,' whispered Cath, loudly enough for them to hear.

'Don't stick your nose in, posh cow. She can answer herself, can't she?'

Amita shrugged her shoulders and settled to her work. Brian's mates continued to make comments to both her and Cath in voices low enough for Mrs Soames to ignore. She was relieved when the session ended and they finally could escape to their last lesson.

Chapter Two
Our own People

'Where do you live?' asked Cath at the end
of the afternoon.

'It's about twenty minutes walk away,'
said Amita, explaining where it was. 'But
my uncle's meeting me today so that I don't
get lost.'

'It's just down the road from me. What's
your uncle's name?'

'Javin Desari. He's my dad's younger brother. He's lived in Southampton about two years now.'

'He runs a business selling to Asian shops doesn't he? My dad knows him quite well.'

Amita didn't want to start talking about her family. She liked Cath but she wasn't sure she'd really understand.

'Tell me about Brian and his gang,' she said to change the subject. 'How come he's so racist when he's black?'

'It's not about race with Brian,' explained Cath. 'It's about living in Southampton. Brian's dad's family were from the Caribbean but they've been here for years and years. Because Southampton's a port there's always been a changing community and some families think they're special. Brian's dad's like that. It's worse because Brian's mum ran off with an Asian

15

guy about three years ago, so he really hates Asians.'

Amita thought about it. She supposed it made some sort of sense.

'Don't let Brian get to you. It's just words with him. But you need to watch out for Tony. He's a real menace. He was cautioned by the police last year for carrying a knife in the street. People say he's into drugs. Anyway, see you tomorrow?'

Cath waved at Amita and went off down the road.

Amita looked round. She wasn't sure where she was supposed to wait. Oh no! Luke and Maddy were heading her way. She didn't want to have to face them again. Then she spotted Uncle Javin's car. Rajeeb was with him, looking very pleased with himself. She supposed it was because of the car. Rajeeb was impressed by cars like their uncle's.

She ran over to the car and got in quickly. She didn't notice the nasty look Maddy gave her.

Rajeeb was Amita's elder brother. He had been really pleased when it had been decided that they would move to Southampton to live with their uncle. He knew his uncle had always been the one with ideas. Just look at the way he had built up the new business. It was only two years since he'd moved and he'd got a big house and a flash car. He employed six men and a secretary. He'd come a long way since the corner shop he'd run with Dad.

Javin was fond of his niece and nephew. He wasn't married. He had been once, but things hadn't gone well. That was one of the reasons he'd moved away. He was fond of his brother, Gayan, and had done all he could to help when Amita and Rajeeb's mother had died, but living with him was another thing. They'd only moved down a few weeks ago and already the disagreements were starting again. Gayan had never been a good businessman, and Javin just didn't want his comments and advice.

'How did it go then?' Javin asked.

'OK. I suppose.' Amita shrugged her shoulders, then grinned, 'Yeah, not bad. Most of the teachers are ok and there's this girl, Cath, who's in most of my sets. She says her dad knows you.'

'What's his name?'

'Davis, but I don't know his first name. They live quite close to you.'

'Close to *us*,' said her uncle. 'It's your home now too. Yes, I know Mark Davis quite well. He's a good businessman.'

Rajeeb couldn't wait any longer. He

burst out with his own news.

'Uncle's given me a job too.'

'Driving a delivery van like Dad?'

'No. Much better. I'm going to go round to shops and restaurants and get them to buy from us. I'm going to be the official company rep. And I get to use the car.'

'That's great, Rajeeb!'

Amita was really pleased for her brother, but she wondered what her father would think about it, if the job really was better than his. Family life was just so complicated sometimes.

When they got home her father was already waiting.

'Well? What did you do? Do they make you work hard? What's the discipline like?'

'Give her a chance, Gayan,' laughed Javin. 'You know the school's got a good reputation. I'm sure she will work just as hard as always. The important thing is for her to make friends, and she seems to be doing that. Cath Davis is a nice girl, and they live quite close.'

'I don't want her making friends with white girls. She'd have been better off staying where we were if she's going to do that. At least there were plenty of our own people there.'

'Dad!' Rajeeb and Amita spoke together.

'Cath's really nice – I'm going to be friends with her and you can't stop me!'

Javin tried to calm things down.

'Gayan, how ever are you going to settle with that sort of attitude? There are children from all sorts of places in that school; and they're all working together.'

'You don't understand! Any of you! I don't want my daughter mixing with these racists and that's final. You make friends with our own people or you don't make friends at all!'

Chapter Three
Louts

It was a cold night. Freezing fog pooled round the orange street lights, forming giant traffic cones along the street. Amita had been glad to get to bed. Her father had eventually shut up about Cath, but it had been a difficult evening.

She found it hard to sleep. All the experiences of the day went round and round in her head. Would Southampton work out for all of them? Could her father really settle down after what had happened to the shop?

She heard voices outside in the street. Loud, drunk voices, laughing and singing. For a moment, Amita felt a rising terror. She started to shake with fear. Plucking up courage, she slipped out of bed and peered out of the window. Two young men were winding their way down the street. She could see their football scarves quite clearly as they passed under the lights.

She forced herself to calm down. They were harmless. She was being silly. It couldn't happen here!

Suddenly she heard doors banging inside the house, and her father yelling.

'Call the police! We need help! Javin! Call the police I say!'

Amita pulled on her dressing gown and rushed out of her room. Her father's bedroom was at the front of the house too. He must have been woken by noises outside.

He was cowering at the top of the stairs. Rajeeb was arriving, with Uncle Javin close behind. Amita pushed forward. Her brother was hopeless in situations like this.

'Dad, Dad. It's OK. There's nothing wrong. It was just two men walking past, that's all.'

'It won't happen here, Gayan,' said Javin. 'This is a respectable neighbourhood. They don't do things like that.'

But Gayan wouldn't be reassured.

'I saw them. I heard them. Football hooligans, louts. Screaming and laughing.'

Amita tried to take control of the situation.

'Rajeeb, go and make tea for us all.

I'll stay with Dad.'

She gently pushed her father back into his room and shut the door.

'Dad. Listen to me. It was bad luck before. They built the new football stadium and the shop was on the way to the station. It could have happened to anyone.'

'But it happened to *us*. It was the end of everything!'

'I know that, but we're here now and we can make a new start.'

'Not while there are racist louts around.'

'It's quiet again now. It was just some young men coming home. There's nothing to worry about. We're safe here.'

The tea arrived, and the family sat drinking it together. Gayan felt ashamed, but he just couldn't help himself. He knew Amita was right, but that only made it worse. He had looked foolish in front of his

brother and his children. Javin was a
success, he was a failure. Even as a father.

It was the week before half-term. There was a
light covering of snow on the path. As Amita
and Cath walked through the school gates
a lump of soggy snow hit her on the head.

'Ugh!' She looked round. Luke Castle
was standing laughing at her.

'Too cold for you then? Why don't you
go home to where it's warmer?'

Usually she ignored them but the snow
rapidly melting and dripping down her
neck annoyed her.

'It's colder there than here,' she said.
'Don't you even know where Lancashire is?'

'Who cares? Go back to India!'

That was Maddy.

'Go home. Go home! We don't want
you here!'

'Forget it.' Cath took her arm. 'They're just so stupid.'

Maddy heard her.

'Who're you calling stupid? Just 'cos you've got a big house you think you're so clever.'

Cath and Amita were facing their tormentors. They hadn't seen Brian and Tony appear round the corner.

Suddenly three more snowballs were flung in their direction. Two missed but Amita turned to see where they were coming from. The third hit her hard in the face.

A sharp stone had been hidden in a thin covering of icy slush. She screamed as the blood started to flow from a cut just below her eye.

'Move it!' yelled Tony.

'We'll get you later,' shouted Maddy, as they disappeared out of sight.

Mrs Soames was on gate duty. Strictly speaking, snowball fighting was against school rules, but she had been ignoring it; after all, lots of people were mucking around. But when she heard Amita's scream she hurried over.

Mrs Soames was kindly, but she always saw the best in everyone. All too often she let the wrong people get away with things. She listened to what Cath and Amita told her, and sent them off to the school office to be mopped up. At break-time she sent for them. They went back to the tutor room, where they found Brian and the rest waiting with the teacher.

'Now. We're going to sort this out once and for all,' she said firmly.

'Brian, you must know how stupid it is to put stones in snowballs. Apologise to Catherine and Amita.'

Brian smiled nastily at Amita. 'I'm so sorry,' he smirked. 'I was only messing about. I didn't think.'

The teacher looked pleased. She couldn't see the faces of the others. Tony was making rude gestures. Luke was glaring. Maddy was mouthing something but Amita couldn't work out what it was.

Mrs Soames gave her usual lecture. After a few minutes she sent everyone except Cath and Amita away.

'Brian has apologised. I do understand how hurtful it is to you, but I would like it if you accepted it and made an effort to be friendly. You mustn't take it personally.'

She smiled happily as they left the room. Problem solved. Or so she thought.

Chapter Four
Leave my Daughter Alone!

Of course things didn't get any better.

'Mrs Soames really believes all this stuff she comes out with,' said Cath. 'The best thing we can do is try to keep out of their way.'

That wasn't as easy as it sounded. Brian didn't like being made to apologise and the group went out of their way to make things difficult for Cath and Amita. At first, it was small things, like taking their books and pushing them as they walked past. Then things began to get more threatening. They started following Amita and Cath home. They shouted abuse. They threw things.

Cath and Amita were glad when half-term arrived. They met every day. Amita told her dad she was going to the library to study; it was easier than going through all the arguments again. She really liked Cath. She liked Cath's family too. Her mum was a primary school teacher so she was on holiday as well. Her dad, Mark, worked with computers. He was a consultant who helped businesses install new systems. He knew Uncle Javin quite well.

Amita met Cath's brother Rob a couple of times and wasn't sure about him at first. He was big and tough looking. His hair was

very short and he always wore his
Southampton FC scarf. He was a keen
supporter and liked to wear the 'uniform'.

'He likes to make people think he's
hard,' Cath had said. 'But he's just a big
softie really.'

Amita soon discovered he was also kind
and friendly. He was at sixth-form college
and was very clever. He was going to
university in the autumn.

'Me, I like everybody,' he said. 'Except
Pompey supporters of course. Now they're
real scum!'

'What's a Pompey supporter?' Amita had
asked Cath the first time she'd heard Rob
say this.

'Portsmouth football team,' explained
Cath. 'Southampton and Pompey hate
each other.'

'Does he get involved in the fighting?'

asked Amita nervously. She knew what her dad thought of football fans.

Cath laughed. 'No, it's all an act. He hates any sort of violence. One of his best mates is a Pompey supporter! But because he's so big no one ever tries it on with him.'

Amita had grown to trust Cath. One afternoon when they were alone she talked to her about why they had moved.

'Dad's the eldest so he inherited the business. He and Uncle Javin used to fight a lot, but my gran insisted they worked together.'

'Why did your uncle move away then?'

'After Gran died there was a big row. Uncle Javin said Dad had no idea about how to run a business, so he left to come here.'

'What happened then?'

'Well, it wasn't really Dad's fault. He

could run the shop fine. Rajeeb helped him. The problem was that one of the big stores took over the petrol station nearby.'

'Why did that matter?'

'They opened a shop as well. They sold things cheaper than we did and took away all our trade.'

Amita paused. Even now the memory of what had happened upset her terribly. It was difficult, very difficult, to talk about it – even to Cath.

'Most of the time I was at school so I didn't realise what was going on. The business going down, and all that. But then the attacks started. It was some of the local football fans. They'd opened a new stadium just down the road and the shop was on the way from the station. Dad refused to sell them alcohol before one match and the local thugs decided to make him pay for it.

'They began by walking past the shop and shouting things. It was mostly late in the afternoons, when it was dark. Then they started coming at night and breaking windows. The police came but they couldn't find out who it was.'

Cath saw tears come into Amita's eyes.

'You don't have to tell me if it still upsets you.'

'I want to tell you. I haven't been able to tell anyone before. It was November the fifth. There had been a social evening at school. Rajeeb came with me. Dad wouldn't come. He didn't want to leave the shop.

'We heard the fire engines as we walked home, but we never guessed where they were going. When we got home it was already too late.'

Amita was shaking as she recreated the terrible events in her mind.

'He wasn't there when we got back. Everything was horrible. The worst was the smell. We thought he was dead. He was in hospital but it took ages to find him. He wasn't badly hurt but everything changed.'

Amita was sobbing uncontrollably now, tears running down her cheeks.

'Dad's so scared now. For weeks afterwards he had nightmares, screaming in his sleep. He just hates football fans and he's convinced that everyone who isn't Asian is a racist and out to get him.'

'Can I tell Mum about it?' asked Cath.

'Not about how Dad is, but the rest, if you want to.'

Mrs Davis didn't say anything to Amita, but she was kinder than ever.

'You can come and see us any time you want,' she said. 'Why don't you come for the night sometimes?'

'I'd love to but Dad wouldn't like it.'

It was a relief to be able to say that without a load of questions. Amita was glad that Cath had explained things.

All too soon half-term ended. Cath was worried. She could put up with Brian Willets and his gang but she was anxious about Amita.

Monday wasn't bad, and Cath thought perhaps they had got fed up with picking on them. Brian had been obnoxious in tutor time, but he'd been picking on a couple of new girls. They weren't Asian but they were obviously Muslim. They had come from Iraq. Brian and Tony were going through their whole boring bit again. The girls didn't speak good English and didn't really respond. When Mrs Soames told the boys off they gave her a load of cheek and got sent out.

'Some things just don't change,' whispered Cath.

Cath walked home with Amita. They were halfway there before they heard the row. They didn't even need to look to see who it was.

Maddy ran at Amita, swinging her heavy bag at her. Amita staggered as it hit her in the ribs. Brian was close by and tripped her so she fell heavily on the ground. Tony was laughing and jeering while Luke lifted his foot to kick at her. She twisted away and the kick, aimed at her head, caught her on the shoulder.

Cath ran to help Amita, but Tony was waiting. He grabbed her round the waist.

'Stop that! Stop it now!'

Amita hardly recognised the voice. She heard heavy steps, running, and was aware that Luke and Brian had gone. She heard other feet, running in the opposite direction. Her brother bent to help her up. Her father had grabbed Cath.

'Racist bully! I saw you! I saw you all! I know you; you won't get away with this.'

'Dad! No! Cath's my friend.'

'I've told you before. You can't make friends with these people.' He turned back to Cath.

'Get away. Leave my daughter alone. Leave us all alone.'

Chapter Five
Bodyguards

Cath ran home. She was crying now, although she wouldn't have done in front of Brian and his gang. She understood why Mr Desari had reacted that way, but it hurt her to be accused of racism just because she was white. It wasn't fair.

The back door banged and, before she could head upstairs out of the way Rob came into the room.

'What's up, Cath?'

She hadn't meant to make a fuss about things, and if it had been her mum or dad she wouldn't have said anything. But Rob was different. She explained what had happened.

'I've got some study leave from college,' he said. 'I'll be around after school if you want.'

Cath nodded. 'That would be good, just for a while.'

Amita had had a hard time. Although she hadn't been badly hurt her dad had wanted to go to the police.

'Leave it, Dad. If you do that it will just make everything worse. I wasn't expecting it, that's all. I'll just keep out of their way in future.'

'I'll go to the school then. I'll talk to your teachers about that Davis girl.'

'How many more times? Cath's my friend. She was trying to help me.'

At first her dad wouldn't listen. But in the end he was forced to accept Cath hadn't been involved. He had been wrong again. Wrong, wrong. That made him feel worse.

But he had to have the final word.

'Maybe that girl was trying to help. But you see what happens when you get friendly with white girls? They bring trouble with them! From now on, Rajeeb or myself will meet you every day from school.'

Amita was worried about Cath. After what her dad had said to her, she was frightened that she wouldn't want anything to do with her. But Cath was waiting for her as she got to school.

'We don't have to worry about home

time,' she told Amita. 'Rob's coming to meet us.'

'So's Rajeeb,' Amita laughed. 'We'll have good bodyguards.'

They didn't have any problems with Brian during the day. But at the end of school the group were waiting outside.

At the same time they saw Rajeeb and Rob standing chatting together. When they came over to meet the girls Brian and co just faded away.

'I didn't know you two knew each other,' said Cath.

'Yeah – we met at an open day at college,' said Rajeeb. 'You know Uncle Javin wants me to sign up for a computer course.'

'Who cares about computers?' said Rob. 'Much more important – I've persuaded him to support Southampton. I'm getting him a scarf!'

Amita looked at them in horror.

'What will Dad say?'

'What's it do with him? I'm just going to go to a few games. What he doesn't know won't hurt him.'

Things weren't too bad at school for a while. Cath and Amita were able to avoid *them* most of the time. It was just in the tutor periods when the verbal abuse continued. With Amita's father, or one or other of their brothers around at the end of the day, they didn't get any hassle on the way home.

At home things were more difficult for Amita. Her father was even stricter about where she went and what she was doing and who she was with. He wouldn't let her out without an inquisition.

He was quarrelling with Javin again too.

He hated being a van driver. In the end Javin told him not to bother.

'You're too old to change. Just leave the business to me. You can retire.'

'How can we live with you if I'm not working? I don't want charity.'

'It's not charity. You're family. Anyway Rajeeb is doing well for me. You can rely on him.'

But that wasn't what Gayan wanted to hear. It made him feel even worse. He was at home now with nothing to do or think about except his own bad luck.

Rajeeb had done very well as the rep, and had brought a lot of new business into the company. But Uncle Javin wanted him to take on the computer side of the business as well. He had bought a new computer for Rajeeb, who was supposed to be studying hard on his computer course, but wasn't.

He was spending time with Rob and his friends instead. Rajeeb played computer games sometimes, and would use it to surf the net, but he wasn't keen on working on the sorts of things Javin wanted.

'Spreadsheets are so boring,' he said, getting up from the PC. 'I can't understand this manual at all.'

He went out leaving the computer on.

Gayan got up with a sigh to switch it off, then sat down at it instead. He had always liked computers and couldn't see why Rajeeb had a problem with them. He had thought about trying some writing. He could write an article for the local paper, something about football hooligans, or street crime.

He looked at the spreadsheet on the screen and picked up the manual. Maybe he could work out how to use it. Then he could show Rajeeb something after all. At least, it would give him something useful to do.

Chapter Six
Something's Got to be Done

Cath had been off school for a few days.
Rob still turned up to see Amita safely
home. Rajeeb was meant to be there. He
had promised his father he would look after
his sister, but more and more often he
didn't bother.

'Cath's got 'flu,' said Rob. 'She'll be off

school for the rest of the week. Look, I've got a meeting with my tutor after college tomorrow. Will you be OK if I don't meet you after school?'

Amita shivered. There was a very cold wind blowing.

'Yeah – it should be all right. They haven't been too bad lately. I think they've given up on me. There are new people in the class they can pick on.'

Rob looked at her carefully. He wanted to be sure she meant what she was saying. He saw how cold she looked.

'Here, wear my scarf until you get home.' He wrapped it round her neck and took her hand in his to warm it.

They were only a few metres from Amita's house when her father appeared. He must have been looking for her out of the window.

'Get away from my daughter! Thug! Lout! Hooligan!'

Rob was taken aback.

'Hang on, mate…'

'Go, Rob, leave him to me.' Amita pushed Rob towards his house and turned to her father.

'Dad, he's Cath's brother. He's my friend too.'

Gayan turned on Amita and snatched the football scarf from her neck.

'What do you think you're doing? Wearing this thing!'

He flung the scarf into the gutter and for a moment Amita thought he was going to stamp on it.

'You know what they are like. He's one of them. They never stop.'

Rajeeb arrived at that moment.

'What's up now?'

'Your sister. She's got a boyfriend. A white thug. Why weren't you there to see her home?'

'I do have a job to do, you know. Why don't you go?'

Rajeeb looked at Amita. She pulled a face at him.

'It was Rob,' she said. 'I met him on the way home.'

Her face warned Rajeeb not to say anything to upset their father any more.

'Come on Dad, come inside. We can talk about it then. Let's hear what Amita has to say.'

Gayan looked at them helplessly. He moved slowly back towards the door. Amita thought that he was beginning to look like an old man.

Rajeeb stooped and picked up Rob's scarf. He stuffed it out of sight into his pocket.

Inside Gayan rounded on Amita again.

'How can you shame me in this way?'

'Dad, he's not a thug, he's not my boyfriend, he's nice and he's a friend. I told you, he was just seeing me home.'

But her father wouldn't listen. All the bitterness he had been keeping hidden came out now. How he hated it here, how he hated the people, and how his brother was preventing him from being a success.

Rajeeb and Amita tried to reason with him but he wouldn't listen. Shocked, they saw he had tears in his eyes. Deep down he knew he was in the wrong again but he couldn't admit it. In the end he refused to talk any more and stamped off to his own room.

'Why don't you explain about the bullying at school?' Rajeeb asked.

'Because he will just make it worse.

Anyway it's better now. They've stopped following us.'

The following afternoon it was raining. Amita looked hopefully for her brother at the school gate. After what happened yesterday, maybe he would show up. But there was no one waiting for her, and she set off for home by herself. She was holding her umbrella well down over her head. She had barely gone two hundred metres before she realised Tony and Luke were behind her.

'Gotcha now! No one around to look after you today.' Tony's voice sounded very loud in her ear.

Running sounds. Maddy and Brian appeared in front of her, blocking her way.

'No one to help you now.' Maddy thrust her face close to Amita. Too close.

Amita lashed out with her umbrella.

'Go away! Leave me alone!'

Suddenly there was a ripping sound. Tony had grabbed her umbrella from her and was ripping at it with a knife.

He waved the knife at her. 'Oh yes. We'll leave you alone all right. But not until we've finished with you.'

Luke had grabbed her arms. Brian was looming over her. Maddy was swinging her bag. Round and round, nearer and nearer.

Amita screamed. Louder than she had ever screamed before. More running footsteps. Amita tried to pull her arms free. What now?

Suddenly a large figure in a football scarf loomed up behind Brian and Tony. Crack! Tony and Brian's head made sudden, violent contact. Tony dropped the knife. Maddy dropped her bag and started running. Tony and Brian tried to follow her, but Rob was hanging on to both of them by the collar. Luke thought he'd try and help his friends, took one look at Rob, thought better of it, and scarpered. Eventually Brian and Tony wrenched themselves free and fled.

A car door slamming. More running feet. Amita's legs wouldn't hold her up any longer and she dropped onto the wet paving.

An arm went round her shoulders. But it wasn't Rob.

'Come on, everything's all right now.'

She looked up.

'Dad?'

At last everything was sorted out. Rob explained that his meeting had been cancelled so he came along anyway, although he was a bit late. Gayan had arrived at the same time as Rob. He had seen everything.

It was hard for Gayan to say it, but he knew he had to.

'Young man, I am grateful to you. I apologise for the way I spoke to you before. I see now that I was wrong. Nevertheless, I must make it clear. I will not have you seeing my daughter.'

Rob rarely got angry, but this time it was all too much.

'Look Mr Desari. First off, I am not seeing your daughter. I have my own girlfriend, thank you very much. And another thing. How long are you going to let this go on before you do something? This time something's got to be done.'

Gayan looked at Rob. 'What do you mean, this time? What has been going on?'

Chapter Seven
Just a Game

Someone had called the police. The scene
in the street was chaos for a while but
eventually everything got sorted out. While
they were waiting Amita and Rob
explained everything to her father.

'You are quite right to protect your
sister,' Gayan said to Rob. 'I only wish my
own son was as loyal.'

Suspicion flashed in his eyes again. 'But *your* sister does not need protecting. She is a white girl! Are you sure that was not just an excuse...?'

'For what, exactly?' said Rob. 'Mr Desari, look. Whatever you think, it's not just about race. It's about being different. Some people just can't cope with that.'

Gayan pointed at Rob's football scarf.

'All right. I accept I may have misjudged you. But what about this? You carry the symbols of your own hatred around with you.'

'OK. Point taken. But that's just a game...'

'I suppose you think what happened today is just a game too.'

'Of course I don't. Look, I came along to help Amita, not to get a load of grief.'

Gayan glared at him. 'Thank you, but there will be no further need for you to help. I will do things the way I see best.'

Rob shrugged again. He smiled at Amita and moved away to talk to the policewoman.

Eventually they were all allowed to go home. Rob had promised to make a statement to the police later.

Javin and Rajeeb were both there when they got back.

'Where have you been? We were worried about you!'

Gayan looked at his brother.

'I was worried about Amita. I didn't want her meeting that boy again so I went to meet her.'

He turned to Rajeeb.

'This is all your fault! Amita, attacked in the street! If you'd done what you were told this would never have happened!'

'My fault? Look, Dad, I told you. I've got work to do. You're the one sitting around all day.'

If Amita hadn't felt so shocked, she would have been angry, but the last thing she wanted was a family row. She was the one who had been attacked, but no one seemed to care about her. Pride. Being in control. Sometimes she thought her brother was as bad as her dad.

Amita was off school for a couple of days. When she got back, Cath was back too. She was very pleased to see Amita and gave her a hug.

'I wanted to come round and see you. But...'

Amita knew why she felt she couldn't. Dad. If only she could say, 'It's fine now. When Dad saw Rob in the fight, he knew how wrong he'd been. You can come round anytime!'

If only.

At least things were better at school. Tony

was permanently excluded. Carrying a knife was serious and the police were talking about prosecuting. Brian was going to be moved to a different school. Luke and Maddy were excluded too, but for shorter times.

Things were still difficult at home, but there were good signs even there. Rajeeb was still doing well, but by the summer it was clear that the computer side of things wasn't for him. He just couldn't get his head round it. But someone else could – Gayan! He was discovering he had a real knack with computers. He began to take on the computer side of the business. He talked of setting up his own computer business one day. Slowly, slowly, he was becoming more settled, back in control of his life.

Then came the day when Javin invited the entire Davis family round for a meal. Rob couldn't come, but Cath would be there. Amita was anxious. How would her father react?

In the end, it was a great success. Everyone was relaxed, and there was lots of laughter around the table.

At the end of the meal Gayan spoke quietly to Cath's mum.

'Mrs Davis, you have a fine daughter in Cath. I am very pleased that she is Amita's friend.'

Amita had feared that the dinner party would cause more trouble, but it turned out to be a healing moment for her family.

Rajeeb was now at college in Portsmouth. Much to Rob's disgust, he had deserted Southampton football team. He was now a full Pompey supporter.

'There's no choice at my college,' he said. 'If I turn up there wearing a Southampton scarf I'll get slaughtered!'

One day in the autumn, two football supporters, one wearing red, the other blue, stopped under a lamp-post.

'Coming in for a minute?' asked Rajeeb.

'Alright, but I'd better hide the scarf,' said Rob.

'Why? Dad, you mean? Don't worry about him. He's getting quite tolerant, these days. Even with Southampton supporters!'